Phonics Friends

Oliver's Box
The Sound of Short O

The
Child's
World

By Joanne Meier and Cecilia Minden

The Child's World

Published in the United States of America
by The Child's World®
PO Box 326
Chanhassen, MN 55317-0326
800-599-READ
www.childsworld.com

A special thank you to the Sandoval family for modeling for this book.

The Child's World®: Mary Berendes, Publishing Director

Editorial Directions, Inc.: E. Russell Primm, Editorial Director and Project Editor; Katie Marsico, Associate Editor; Judith Shiffer, Associate Editor and School Media Specialist; Linda S. Koutris, Photo Researcher and Selector

The Design Lab: Kathleen Petelinsek, Design and Page Production

Photographs ©: Photo setting and photography by Romie and Alice Flanagan/Flanagan Publishing Services: cover, 4, 8, 12, 14, 16, 18, 20; Punchstock/Comstock: 6; Corbis: 10.

Library of Congress Cataloging-in-Publication Data
Meier, Joanne D.
  Oliver's box : the sound of short O / by Joanne Meier and Cecilia Minden.
    p. cm. — (Phonics friends)
  Summary: Simple text featuring the sound of the short "o" describes a game Oliver loves to play.
  ISBN 1-59296-315-3 (library bound : alk. paper)
[1. English language—Phonetics. 2. Reading.] I. Minden, Cecilia. II. Title. III. Series.
  PZ7.M5148Ol 2004
  [E]—dc22   2004003536

Note to parents and educators:

The Child's World® has created Phonics Friends with the goal of exposing children to engaging stories and pictures that assist in phonics development. The books in the series will help children learn the relationships between the letters of written language and the individual sounds of spoken language. This contact helps children learn to use these relationships to read and write words.

The books in this series follow a similar format. An introductory page, to be read by an adult, introduces the child to the phonics feature, or sound, that will be highlighted in the book. Read this page to the child, stressing the phonic feature. Help the student learn how to form the sound with her mouth. The Phonics Friends story and engaging photographs follow the introduction. At the end of the story, word lists categorize the feature words into their phonic element. Additional information on using these lists is on The Child's World® Web site listed at the top of this page.

Each book in this series has been carefully written to meet specific readability requirements. Close attention has been paid to elements such as word count, sentence length, and vocabulary. Readability formulas measure the ease with which the text can be read and understood. Each Phonics Friends book has been analyzed using the Spache readability formula. For more information on this formula, as well as the levels for each of the books in this series please visit The Child's World® Web site.

Reading research suggests that systematic phonics instruction can greatly improve students' word recognition, spelling, and comprehension skills. The Phonics Friends series assists in the teaching of phonics by providing students with important opportunities to apply their knowledge of phonics as they read words, sentences, and text.

The letter *o* makes two sounds.

The long sound of *o* sounds like *o* as in:

open and *rope.*

The short sound of *o* sounds like *o* as in:

job and *box.*

In this book, you will read words that
have the short *o* sound as in:

box, frog, dog, and *pop.*

Oliver has a box.

He likes to play a game.

Can you guess what

is in the box?

It can hop a lot.

It can jump a lot.

It is a frog!

It is soft.

It can sleep in a box.

Some are named Spot.

It is a dog!

You can drop this.

It will not pop.

It is a balloon!

It is not a pet. It is small.

You find it on the street.

It is a rock!

Oliver loves to play this game.

You are doing a great job!

Keep going!

It can be hot. Mother takes the top off. It is a pot!

Oliver's box has one more thing. It has hands. It can tell time. It is a clock!

Oliver loves his box.

You can have a box, too!

What is in your box?

Fun Facts

You might think that most boxes are only used for packing things or for storing your toys. But some boxes can actually make music! The first music box was probably invented in Switzerland in 1770. They were a popular way to play music until the early 1900s, when the phonograph was invented.

The Goliath frog of West Africa is one big amphibian! This frog often grows to be the size of the average house cat. The highest a frog has ever jumped in a single leap is 17.5 feet (5.3 meters). Although frogs have lungs, they actually breathe through their skin. Some kinds of frogs can live to be 40 years old.

Activity

Building a Riddle Box
Are you good at solving riddles? How about your friends? Test your knowledge by building a riddle box. Seal a cardboard box and have an adult help you cut a hole in the top. Write riddles on small slips of paper and drop them through the hole. Have your friends take turns picking riddles out of the box. Whoever answers the most correctly gets to create the riddles that will be used for the next round.

To Learn More

Books
About the Sound of Short O
Flanagan, Alice K. *Hot Pot: The Sound of Short O*. Chanhassen, Minn.: The Child's World, 2000.

About Boxes
Fleming, Candace, and Stacey Dressen McQueen (illustrator). *Boxes for Katie*. New York: Farrar, Straus and Giroux, 2003.

Morrison, Toni, Slade Morrison, and Giselle Potter (illustrator). *The Big Box*. New York: Hyperion Books for Children, 1999.

About Dogs
Klingel, Cynthia, and Robert B. Noyed. *Dogs*. Chanhassen, Minn.: The Child's World, 2001.

Rylant, Cynthia. *Dog Heaven*. New York: Blue Sky Press, 1995.

About Frogs
Baker, E. D. *The Frog Princess*. New York: Bloomsbury, 2002.

Wilson, Karma, and Joan Rankin (illustrator). *A Frog in the Bog*. New York: Margaret K. McElderry Books, 2003.

Web Sites
Visit our home page for lots of links about the Sound of Short O:
http://www.childsworld.com/links.html

Note to Parents, Teachers, and Librarians: We routinely check our Web links to make sure they're safe, active sites—so encourage your readers to check them out!

Short O
Feature Words

Proper Names
Oliver
Spot

Feature Words in
Medial Position
box
clock
dog
drop
frog
hop
hot
job
lot
not
pop
pot
rock
soft
top

About the Authors

Joanne Meier, PhD, has worked as an elementary school teacher and university professor. She earned her BA in early childhood education from the University of South Carolina, and her MEd and PhD in education from the University of Virginia. She currently works as a literacy consultant for schools and private organizations. Joanne Meier lives with her husband Eric, and spends most of her time chasing her two daughters, Kella and Erin, and her two cats, Sam and Gilly, in Charlottesville, Virginia.

Cecilia Minden, PhD, directs the Language and Literacy Program at the Harvard Graduate School of Education. She is a reading specialist with classroom and administrative experience in grades K–12. She earned her PhD in reading education from the University of Virginia. Cecilia and her husband Dave Cupp enjoy sharing their love of reading with their granddaughter Chelsea.